D0473510

Party Time, All the Time!

by Sue Gonzalez

Grosset & Dunlap
An Imprint of Penguin Group (USA) Inc.

© 2010 Disney. All rights reserved. Used under license by Penguin Young Readers Group.
Published by Grosset & Dunlap, a division of Penguin Young Readers Group, 345 Hudson Street, New York, New York 10014.
GROSSET & DUNLAP is a trademark of Penguin Group (USA) Inc. Manufactured in China.

Library of Congress Control Number: 2010005980

ISBN 978-0-448-45456-6   10 9 8 7 6 5 4 3 2 1

Come on in!
The Party's Starting

Get stoked for a look back at the best Club Penguin parties. It's all about what happened, who was there, and what the penguins did to make each Club Penguin party an event to remember. Each party had some kind of theme that made it one-of-a-kind and unforgettable.

Put on your favorite party hat or your best silly glasses. Set out plenty of food and water for your puffle. Leave your igloo for a little while and come with us on a trip back in time as we remember all the most awesome parties in Club Penguin history.

Waddle on!
The Club Penguin Team

ONE-OF-A-KIND CLUB PENGUIN EVENTS

You never know what to expect next on Club Penguin. Every day is a blast on this snowy island. It's a place where fun and friendship are a way of life. But certain events have been extra special. Take a look at some penguin openings and party moments that we'll never forget.

Club Penguin's First Party Ever
The Beta Test Party

When Club Penguin was just starting out, the first penguins to try out the games and other fun stuff on Club Penguin were called Beta Testers. They reported to the Club Penguin Team about any problems they found.

To thank the Beta Tester penguins, the Club Penguin Team threw Club Penguin's very first party—the Beta Test Party. It was Club Penguin's Grand Opening held in the Town Center!

The famous yellow and pink striped Beta Party Hat was given away at Club Penguin's first party. The original Club Penguin Beta Testers can still be seen proudly wearing this hat—it is a sign that they were among the very first penguins on the island. The Beta Party Hat is one of the most prized items on the island but has never been given away since.

Club Penguin Is Up and Running!
Server Testing Giveaways

To thank every Beta Penguin who helped test the servers, Club Penguin launched the Server Testing Giveaways. Penguins collected cool free stuff, like black bowties and red and blue sunglasses.

The Cove Opening

One day in year two, a penguin was playing *Jet Pack Adventure* and revved the engine up too high! He lost control and crash-landed on an undiscovered part of the island. Hearing the crash of ocean surf, this brave penguin went to explore. That's when the Cove was discovered.

The Cove opened in May of year two with a splash. To celebrate this brand-new beach spot, penguins threw a three-day party. They surfed and swam. They played the new surf game *Catchin' Waves* at the Surf Hut. They also got lifeguard whistles as a giveaway item.

The Underground Opening

It all started when explorer penguins found caves that led underground. It was amazing—a world of passages and caves. They soon went to work rebuilding the caves and tunnels so other penguins could use them safely.

When the Underground was finally finished, it was time to celebrate. Penguins everywhere received free hard hats and helmets as giveaways at the Underground Opening.

Cart-Surfer was also revealed at this party! Penguins shot down dark underground tunnels on old mining carts and let the good times roll.

An Interview with Aunt Arctic

Aunt Arctic, editor in chief for *The Club Penguin Times*, has been covering the Club Penguin scene almost since the beginning. It was around the time of the Underground Opening that she wrote her first article for the paper!

Usually, Aunt Arctic is the one who does the interviews. But this time, Club Penguin is interviewing her:

Club Penguin: Aunt Arctic, you've been covering events on the island since the very beginning. What is one of the most exciting events you've covered?

Aunt Arctic: I loved covering the first Penguin Play Awards. It was so thrilling. All the plays were wonderful! And the starring penguins were so glamorous. No one could predict who would win.

CP: What do you like to do for fun?

AA: I love taking my adorable puffles for walks. And even though it's technically my job, I have lots of fun helping penguins by answering their questions in my column "Ask Aunt Arctic."

CP: Do you consider yourself something of a Club Penguin historian?

AA: Well, I know a lot about the island from covering so many events. But even I don't know everything there is to know! There's always something new and exciting happening here. And I'm here to cover it all!

A Beacon of Light
The Lighthouse Grand Opening Party

Down at the Beach, the Lighthouse had fallen into disrepair. Thanks to hardworking penguins and the Restore the Lighthouse event, where kids could donate to a fund to help repair it, the Lighthouse was opened to the public for the first time. Penguins who donated seven hundred fifty coins to pay for the Lighthouse received a red and white striped T-shirt.

The big Lighthouse Grand Opening was reason to celebrate. A red sailor's cap was the free giveaway at the three-day party.

With its new stage, the Lighthouse was the perfect place for a concert. The Club Penguin Band played and many other penguin musicians have been playing there ever since.

S.O.S.—Save Our Ship!

The Save the *Migrator* Campaign
and Captain Rockhopper and Yarr's *Arr*-ival Party

Shiver me timbers! Captain Rockhopper's ship, the *Migrator*, hit an iceberg and sank. Penguins watched from the shore as Captain Rockhopper and his first mate, Yarr, rowed safely away. But was this the end of the *Migrator*? No way! Loyal penguins dived right in to help.

Gary the Gadget Guy started the Save the *Migrator* Campaign. He created the Aqua Grabber which grabbed pieces of the wreckage from the ocean floor. Divers went below the sea to repair the ship. When it was all fixed, the Aqua Grabber grabbed the *Migrator* and pulled it up.

To thank his penguin friends, Captain Rockhopper threw a party on board. The Crow's Nest was opened, and Captain Rockhopper gave away the key to the Captain's Quarters. *Avast, me hearties*. It was a piratey good time!

THE DOJO GRAND OPENING

In Club Penguin's early days, the Dojo was a building full of mystery hidden in the mountains. Then, the Dojo was struck by lightning, creating a hole in the room.

But penguins got to work rebuilding it. Soon, the new Dojo Courtyard was revealed. And a new game, *Card-Jitsu*, helped penguins train to earn their colored belts and become ninjas.

To show his thanks, the mysterious Sensei made his public debut, opening the Dojo with a big bash in November of year four.

A Penguin with All the Right Moves
An Interview with Sensei

Determined reporter Aunt Arctic was able to get a rare interview with Sensei. This wise, gray penguin trains penguins to become ninjas.

Aunt Arctic: Some say you hide away here in the Dojo. How do you feel about that?

Sensei: The wisest penguin knows that ninjas are hidden only in their hearts.

AA: That's a bit hard to understand. Why do you speak in haiku?

S: It's quite easy to sound very sage and wise speaking with haikus.

AA: Many say you're a penguin of mystery. How would you describe yourself?

S: Like the pebbles of a riverbed that steer the rapids toward the sea, Sensei is at once easily understood and profoundly bemusing.

AA: Thank you for your time, Sensei.

S: Sensei is happy to speak with you. Sensei vanish!

AA: Hey, where did he go? Well, that's Sensei for you—you never know when he'll pop in . . . or out.

UNFORGETTABLE ANNIVERSARY PARTIES

Club Penguin's anniversary comes every year on October 24. To celebrate, penguins throw a big party at the Coffee Shop. Each year, penguins get a new party hat and a new pin.

Penguins like to look back on all the fun of the year before. They place a brand-new yearbook in the Book Room to honor each year's special events. Awesome!

A *One*-derful Year

1 DAY ONLY

Club Penguin's first year seemed to go by so fast. No one could believe it! The first anniversary party hat was green and blue. (It is considered the second rarest item on Club Penguin. The rarest is the Beta Party Hat.)

Captain Rockhopper pulled into port and joined in. And there was a huge cake to commemorate the one-year milestone.

Two Too Good To Be True

Club Penguin's anniversary number two came around quickly. Penguins danced wearing yellow and orange party hats. The big anniversary cake got even bigger and featured miniature penguins holding up the layers.

Three's a Crazy, Crowded Blast

Captain Rockhopper shipped in a canon to start off Club Penguin's third anniversary with a bang! Another big cake made the party super delicious. Its bottom layer was a mini-model of the Town Center and the Plaza.

Gary the Gadget Guy invented the Wishmaker 3000, a superbig fan, just for this party. Penguins had to blow the top of the cake off with the Wishmaker 3000 to get the orange, yellow, and dark blue hats that were hidden inside.

Four-ever Fun

For this anniversary party, instead of just *eating* a big cake, the Coffee House was turned *into* a big cake! On the roof were real birthday candles. Inside were free cupcakes, music, beverages, and prizes. Penguins had fun, fun, fun searching for the year's new light blue and purple party hats. They were hidden in a secret place—a piñata.

All the World's a Stage

PENGUIN PLAY AWARDS

The First Annual Penguin Play Awards was held at the Plaza. Penguins voted for five different categories—Best Overall Play, Best Sound, Best Effects, Best Costume, and Best Set.

Penguins gathered at the Plaza to view the results. And the big winner was . . . *The Quest for the Golden Puffle*! While penguins across the island were voting for the awards, a party was held backstage. Aunt Arctic, Gary the Gadget Guy, Cadence, and the Club Penguin Band all gave out autographed backgrounds.

Finders, Keepers
How to Find Special Giveaway Items

One of the many great things about Club Penguin parties is that penguins get some amazing free stuff. Here are some examples of party giveaways:

How can you get these giveaways? Often they are hidden in secret places. Penguins can help each other, too, by giving clues or even by simply telling friends where they found giveaways. So if you see a penguin wearing the latest giveaway, just ask him or her where they found it!

A PARTY FOR EVERY REASON AND EVERY SEASON

Any day is right for a party on Club Penguin. And holidays mean really big celebrations. Here are the most memorable holiday parties in Club Penguin history.

Penguins Make the Green Scene

Penguins rock the color green on St. Patrick's Day. In fact, the whole island is painted green. The famous Shamrock Hat was given away at the first St. Patrick's Day party and on the second as well. In year three, the hat was gigantic!

The fourth St. Patrick's Day party was bigger and better than ever. To participate, you just had to turn yourself green! An accordion was given away, along with a small Shamrock Hat and the Lucky Shamrock coin. The party was held at an awesome Leprechaun House located in the Forest. It could be found by walking into a tree house door. The dance floor at the Night Club flashed yellow and green and then turned into a shamrock! A giant pot of gold sat at the end of a rainbow in the Ski Village.

Silliness soars to new heights at the April Fools' party each year. There wasn't anything sillier than the propeller cap given away at the very first April Fools' Day Party. And for the first time ever in Club Penguin history, penguins could adopt puffles!

That same cap was blue at the second party the following year. It looked especially wacky when worn with that year's other hilarious giveaway—a funny nose and glasses.

The Forest was the place to be on April first in year three. The place was turned upside down when everything was turned wrong side up. And the island was painted in a variety of art styles. That year, a red propeller hat was given away. A penguin could hover above the dance floor by dancing with this hat on! Swirly glasses were also given away.

Year four's April Fools' Day Party brought strange boxes to the island. One of them took you to the Box Dimension, a new room filled with boxes, odd plants, and all-around strangeness. Penguins could only access the dimension from inside their igloos. Penguins still visit the Box Dimension today, but the only way to get in is to find someone with a box and step through the box portal.

Once more, strange boxes appeared all over the island on April first of year five. What was in them? Silly things, of course.

Easter Parties

Penguins donned their free pink bunny ears and collected colorful Easter eggs from all over the island during the first Club Penguin Easter Egg Hunt. Then they generously shared them with their puffles.

The new stage at the Lighthouse was the place for Easter songs in April of the second year. That year, the free bunny ears were blue.

In year three, the giveaway bunny ears were green. Penguins hunted for a special ninja Easter egg. This was very exciting because there were no ninjas yet on Club Penguin. Penguins suspected it was a sign of something exciting to come—and they were right!

Penguins love hunting for clues and figuring out riddles—which is exactly what they did during the Easter Egg Scavenger Hunt in year four! Some penguins showed Easter spirit by putting on bunny costumes. Other penguins stuck with just the ears. Much to the happiness of penguins everywhere, pink bunny ears were given away once again! And they were pink, just like the very first Easter Egg Hunt.

Summer Sizzle
Summer Parties

June was jumpin' on Club Penguin at the first Summer Party. Down at the Beach, the barbecue blazed with sizzling shrimp and fancy fish. The gigantic, blowup octopus at the Dojo made everyone say, "Wow!" And a new penguin game, *Cart Surfer*, made its debut. Many penguins remember this party as one of the greatest in all of Club Penguin history. There were lots of giveaways: water wings, a duck toy, a lifeguard whistle, and a blue Hawaiian lei.

In year two, summer arrived again and penguins once more wanted to kick off their shoes and have fun. At the Summer Kick-Off Party, blue Hawaiian leis were super giveaways. Green sunglasses and a flower headdress made the party summer sweet. Penguins proudly put on their ice cream apron giveaways and kept cool in the summer swelter.

Wet and Wild!
Water Parties

There was water everywhere at the big Water Party held in year one. That was when a crab cracked the glass in the Underground! No one's sure whether it was by accident or on purpose, but luckily, fast-thinking penguins hooked up hoses to drain the flood and save the day. And since they were already wet, they held the Water Party! After a wet and wild time, every penguin waved good-bye, and went home with a fishbowl for a prize.

During the Waddle on Water Party in year two, there were water balloons and water polo—even a big, rubber whale that squirted water down at the Iceberg.

Fall Means Fairs on Club Penguin

In year two, Captain Rockhopper pulled into port loaded with secret cargo. Curious penguins took a peek. Surprise! He had brought everything penguins needed to throw their first-ever Fall Fair.

There was a puffle paddle game and a puffle feeding game called Feed-a-Puffle. There were giveaway cotton candy and lollipops to eat, and free feathered tiaras and candy necklaces to wear. What fabulous fall fun it was! And the coolest thing about this party was that by playing the fair games, penguins could earn tickets that they could redeem for awesome prizes.

At the Fall Fair in year three, giant green and yellow sunglasses were given away. There were delicious giveaway candy apples and candy necklaces, too. This year, the giveaway cotton candy was blue.

There were also new fair games that allowed penguins to win prizes only available during the fair. A cool carrousel made this a fair to remember.

 Captain Rockhopper brought the Great Puffle Circus to the Fall Fair in year four. Trained puffles performed all sorts of amazing tricks for the crowd. There were new giveaways like tiaras and hats.

Penguins LOVE Halloween! The Halloween Party in year one was the first Club Penguin party after the site officially launched. Penguins carved scary pumpkins, strung spidery webs, and did a wacky waddle out on their new dance floor at the Night Club.

In year two, pumpkin lights glowed and every igloo shone with its flickering brightness. Penguins dressed as goblins and ghosts and haunted one another for treats. Everyone received a wizard hat as a giveaway.

On Halloween in year three, an eclipse darkened the skies over the island. Penguins gathered at the Lighthouse to watch a scary movie—*Night of the Living Sled*! And the Forest was changed into a spooky spot. The first yellow puffle was spotted and penguins went on a candy scavenger hunt. Every penguin got a Halloween scarf and a pumpkin basket.

HIDE IN THE SPOOKY FOREST

Crack! Bang! Boom! Lightning and thunder struck on Halloween in year four. Everyone got a giveaway pumpkin basket. And penguins watched *Night of the Living Sled II* at the Dance Lounge.

At the Halloween Party in year five, penguins went to a haunted house where freaky fruit floated in the air, ghostly puffles popped up from nowhere, and penguin pictures popped out of their frames. Penguins also met Gary the Gadget Guy at a black-and-white secret laboratory, where they saw his new invention—the Monster Maker. A special catalog at the secret laboratory featured monster costumes to mix and match.

Penguins also went on a candy scavenger hunt and they watched *Night of the Living Sled III* at the Lighthouse. Everyone received fun pumpkin antennae to wear. It was awful—awfully fun, that is.

Aloha, Penguins
Winter Luau

How low can a Penguin go?! Penguins got down as they waddled under the limbo stick during the Winter Luau held in year one. It was at the Dock, of course. Penguins roasted fish on an open fire and hulaed. The red Hawaiian lei that was given away is still a rare and valued collectible.

WINTER FIESTA!

In year two, at the Winter Fiesta, the island was filled with fun, fiesta frills to help beat the winter blues. Piñatas could be found and maracas were the giveaway item.

 At the fiesta in year two, sombreros and piñatas were everywhere! Penguins broke a special piñata to find a hidden cactus pin within. Everyone got maracas to play.

In January of year three, maracas were once again the giveaway item at the Winter *Fiesta*-val! They had tacos, tortillas, and a terrific time.

In year four, penguins got tiny sombreros to wear! *Ole!*

The Festival of Snow

In year two, the first Festival of Snow sparkled with crystal creations. This winter wonderland of art was created by Gary the Gadget Guy's great invention—the AC 3000 Cooling System, which spread ice everywhere. Inspired ice sculptures dazzled penguins in the winter sun. All penguins received an ice crown and a snowflake T-shirt.

The Freeze Master
An Interview with Gary the Gadget Guy

Aunt Arctic interviewed Gary the Gadget Guy in his workshop, where he remembered the winter he invented the AC 3000 Cooling System.

Aunt Arctic: What inspired you to invent the AC 3000 Cooling System?

Gary the Gadget Guy:
I am deeply fascinated with precipitation in all its manifestations. And, I think it's nice to be able to make ice sculptures whenever you want. With the AC 3000 Cooling System, penguins can have snowball fights in July.

AA: Was there any other reason?

Gary: The functionality of my inventions has wide-reaching implications for creating recreational frozen H_2O over at the Ski Village and at other Club Penguin facilities—plus I really just like inventing.

AA: I had a feeling . . . Thanks for your time.

Ho-Ho-Ho! Let It Snow!

The first Christmas Party was held at the Snow Forts in year one. Over at the Plaza, a giant Christmas tree was set up. Special giveaways included a Santa hat and Santa beard.

Did the snowstorm of year two stop the Christmas Party fun? No way! Dressed as Santa and his elves, penguins and puffles made their Christmas tree shine. That year, the Christmas Party was voted one of the best parties in Club Penguin history.

 Club Penguin's third Christmas Party featured a huge Christmas tree in the Ski Lodge. It reached right up to the attic! But everyone also loved the spindly little Christmas pine on the Iceberg. That year, everyone got a Santa hat, reindeer ears, and a Christmas scarf to wear.

In year four, penguins in elf costumes decked the island in holiday cheer. They strung festive garlands on the *Migrator*, and everyone loved the Christmas lights on the Dojo. A festive Santa hat giveaway made everyone jolly.

Captain Rockhopper sailed into port for the holidays that year. He collected all the Coins for Change that charitable penguins donated.

At the Christmas party in year five, there was a giant tree lit up in the Forest. And, in the Town Center, a toy workshop for elves was set up. Presents were delivered on Santa's sleigh, and you could also send a postcard gift to friends. Best of all, the giveaway item was a white beard—just like Santa's!

Penguin Power

Penguins care! And they prove it each year by participating in the Coins for Change program, which helps children around the world. Coins for Change is all about playing games to earn coins, and then donating coins at stations around the island. You can even choose to donate to a specific cause. Then Club Penguin donates one million dollars among the charities.

In year five, you could choose to help kids who are poor, help kids who are sick, or help the environment. And kids could put donation booths in their igloos and hold fund-raising parties. In addition, that year there was a benefit concert at the Lighthouse!

That's the Club Penguin holiday spirit!

Penguin Party Tips
How to Be In the Know

The What's New blog tells penguins all about upcoming parties. It's a good thing, too, if you want to prepare yourself for the big event.

How can you get ready?

- Buy clothing items or costumes from the Penguin Style catalog that fit the party theme.

- Decorate your igloos in the party theme.

- Get together with friends and play party planner.

- Think about the party, tell your penguin friends about it, and plan to have a great time.

A DREAM OF A THEME

Are you a pizza lover? Is being in the Wild West your favorite fantasy? Do you fancy yourself a medieval knight or princess? No matter what your personality, Club Penguin has thrown a theme party for you. Here are some of the most memorable Club Penguin theme parties.

Pizza Pizzazz
The Pizza Party

Pizza and games—what could be better? Not much! In February of year one, Club Penguin celebrated with a Pizza Party. Penguins received a pizza apron and chef's hat. Everyone played *Pizzatron 3000* and pigged out on pizza.

Yee-Ha!
Western Parties

In July of year one, cowboy and cowgirl penguins stomped to the tune of a penguin line dance and then threw their hats in the air. The Night Club hosted the Western Party complete with hootin', hollerin', and country tunes. Everyone looked rootin' tootin' wearing the free cowboy bandana giveaway.

Penguins voted for year one's best party ever and the Western Party won! And so, in year three, Club Penguin threw a second Western Party—but this time, it was a surprise! The Cove and Dock were decorated with colorful cacti and cactus flowers bloomed in the Forest. The Night Club was stacked with bales of hay and there was a covered wagon parked by the Snow Forts. Wooden rocking horses were hitched to posts at the Plaza. Plus, penguins got cool red bandanas as a giveaway. *Yahoo!*

Lost and Found

The Instrument Scavenger Hunt

In July of year two, musical penguins scoured the island looking for band instruments on a list. The drum was at the Pizza Parlor, the cymbal was at the Dock, and the piano was at the Pet Shop! And that's just to name a few!

As a prize, all penguins who found instruments received a free band player card background.

Seek and You Will Find

The Fiery Fun Scavenger Hunt

Penguins followed Sensei's clues at the Fiery Fun Scavenger Hunt in September of year four.

The sky turned orange and penguins searched for a list of fiery fun stuff to help prepare the Dojo's new Path of Fire. Many penguins found themselves searching for the black puffle, which ignites into flame when a penguin with a ninja mask or ninja suit is near. Penguins who found all the items on the list won an amazing new fire pin.

In addition, if a ninja stood near certain flames around the island, the flame would grow . . . indicating that something was coming!

The penguins held their first Sports Party in August of year one. The Red Team played the Blue Team in ice hockey, and they had a big Sports Party to celebrate. All penguins got red or blue face paint. Naturally every penguin needed free ice skates, too.

In year three, the second Blue and Red Team ice hockey game was held. Once again, penguins got to pick blue or red face paint giveaways. Cool new ways for penguins to race and win medals were featured.

Party on Deck!
The Pirate Party

In May of year three, penguins shouted, "Yo-ho-ho!" Why? Because Captain Rockhopper invited them all into the hold of his ship, the *Migrator*, for the Pirate Party. Everyone got a free sailor's cap.

Lots of penguins threw their own Pirate Parties in their igloos.

Undersea Celebration
The Sub-marine Party

Wearing snorkel gear and mermaid fins, penguins dove right in for the Sub-marine Party. This party wrapped up the Save the *Migrator* Campaign, for which penguins pitched in to restore Captain Rockhopper's beloved ship. The water balloon toss at the Sub-marine Party whet everyone's appetite for further watery festivities. The giant blowup octopus returned and lucky penguins got great giveaways: a seashell belt and a yellow snorkel.

A *Knight* to Remember

Club Penguin's brave knight and fair princess penguins came out for a Medieval Party in year four. A few ferocious dragons arrived, too. (Everyone looked very cool in their costumes.) They built a tree house in the Forest, and wizard hats and squire's tunics were given away.

Castles and fortresses were the highlight of the next Medieval Party, held in year five. Everyone went on a quest to explore the Club Penguin kingdom. Penguins found a maze, fought a dragon hiding in the Mine, and discovered a hidden treasure. Penguins received a golden set of knight's armor, too.

We Be Jammin'

Music Jams came to Club Penguin in year three.

The Club Penguin Band rocked so hard that they nearly cracked the Iceberg. Penguin fans shook the free maracas given away at the event and, to this day, penguins love to wear their Music Jam T-shirts.

After the show, the Club Penguin Band came out to meet their many penguin fans. Their fans love it when Club Penguin Band members go to the backstage area to say hello to them after a show.

In year four, the Lighthouse was the place to play for musical penguins. Lots of penguins started their own bands and performed. Every penguin received green headphones.

Rock, Roll, Slide, and Spin
An Interview with the Club Penguin Band

Aunt Arctic met with GBilly and Franky of the Club Penguin Band to ask them some questions.

Aunt Arctic: What is your favorite memory as a band?

GBilly: Speaking for myself, I really loved playing at the first Penguin Play Awards at the Stage. Some penguins formed their own bands and played during the after party. I loved meeting them backstage.

AA: Any other memories?

Franky: The Music Jam in year four was awesome. The Battle of the Bands rocked! And I loved the different stages set up all around the island. My favorite was the pink one at the Beach.

GBilly: I liked the rooftop stage on the Night Club.

AA: Thanks for speaking with us today, guys.

GBilly: My pleasure.

Franky: Yeah, waddle on.

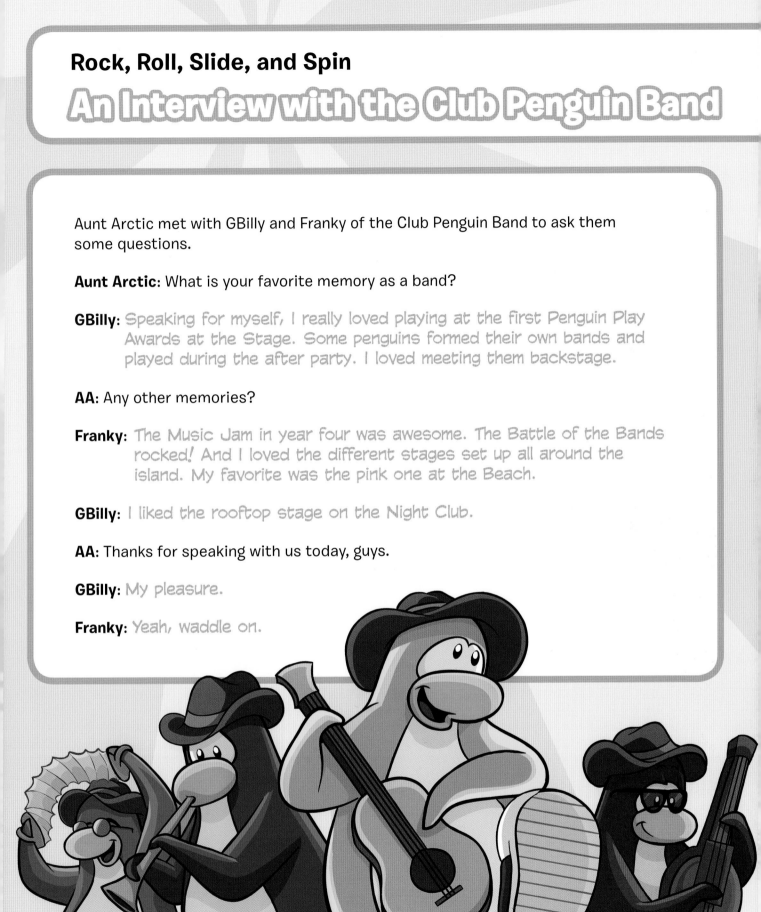

PUFFLE PARTY

Penguins are mad crazy for their pet puffles! So, in year four they celebrated their furry friends. Penguins fed their puffles and tossed snowballs at the Snow Forts. It was such a blast that even the never-before-seen white puffle—who is known to be gentle yet powerful—poked its head out and joined the excitement.

The amazing decorations for this party held a special secret. When penguins took their puffles for walks, the decorations turned the same color as the puffle!

What were those strange plants that arrived when Captain Rockhopper brought the *Migrator* into port in year three? Curious penguins just had to know—and they soon found out! The plants grew so fast they quickly took over the island.

Did the penguins panic?

Of course not!

They threw an Adventure Party and did some exploring. Penguins discovered tropical wildlife, ancient relics, and all sorts of exotic greenery they had never seen before.

The Waddle On Dance-a-Thon

DJ Cadence hosted the Waddle On Dance-a-Thon in year five and penguins rocked the all-new dance floor. Cadence showed penguins a new game called *Dance Contest* and penguins got a supercool boom box that allowed them to break-dance for the first time. They were bustin' moves for days!

DANCE CONTEST

Everybody Dance Now
An Interview with Cadence

Aunt Arctic always interviews the island's most well-known penguins. Here she talks to Cadence, often known as the "Dance Machine."

Aunt Arctic: Cadence, what makes you such a terrific DJ?

Cadence: I so love to see penguins movin' and groovin'. I pick tunes that make them shake their tail feathers. My job is to get them up on the dance floor.

AA: What's your favorite kind of music?

C: Truly, I love it all. I have to run now. It's time to start spinning some tunes.

AA: Thanks for talking with me today. Is there anything you'd like to leave our readers with?

C: Stay cold, everyone. I'll see you on the dance floor.

FESTIVAL OF FLIGHT

Gary the Gadget Guy gave a grand tour of his latest inventions at the Festival of Flight! This was a week-long party. It came about when Gary decided to change the windows in the Underground. To do this, he found a way to float the entire island up into the air!

Penguins got to see Gary's newest invention, the Cloud Maker 3000, on the Ski Hill. It turned images into clouds when the button was pressed. That week, the Cloud Maker 3000 made some cool shapes including an anvil, puffles, the *Migrator*, fish, and a rubber duck!

Lucky penguins put on silly green propeller hats and flew up, up, and away in the hot air balloon! They floated to the highest mountain.

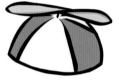

Going Camping
The Camp Penguin Party

In August of year three, penguins went to summer camp! At the Camp Penguin Party, the island was transformed to look just like a real camp! Penguins played the parts of campers and counselors. This party had an incredible giveaway—a marshmallow on a stick! Penguins happily sat by the fire at the Cove, chatting and making delicious toasted marshmallows.

House Party!

How to Throw a Party in Your Igloo

You don't have to wait for a party. Throw your own in your igloo! Here are some tips on how to do it:

- Decorate your igloo. Check out the Better Igloos catalog for banners, balloons, and lights.

- Play music. Better Igloos carries a stereo and a jukebox. Pick a tune that suits you and leave it on.

- Invite guests. You can send postcards to penguins on your buddy list. But, if you want to invite penguins you don't know, open your igloo on the main map by unlocking it.

- If you're not getting guests, go to the Town Center and invite penguins to your party.

- Be a good host. Greet each guest who arrives. Start a dance or a snowball fight. Make sure everyone has a really great time—especially you!

Many More Parties to Come!

Parties make Club Penguin hop and pop. They're the icing on the cake. The next big thing to get stoked about.

And let's not forget all that fun free stuff given away at parties—the cool, one-of-a-kind props that make your penguin stand out.

The Club Penguin Team is always inspired by YOUR ideas. Right now we're planning a lot of awesome new parties—so stay in touch with us on our blog. We totally want to hear what you have to say.

So . . . until next time . . .

Waddle on!
The Club Penguin Team